W9-BKA-705

Clifford's
PUPPY DAYS
NORMAN BRIDWELL

SCHOLASTIC INC.

New York   Toronto   London   Auckland   Sydney

For Christy Jean Stalling

No part of this publication may be reproduced in whole or in part, or stored in a retrieval system, or transmitted in any form or by any means, electronic, mechanical, photocopying, recording, or otherwise, without written permission of the publisher. For information regarding permission, write to Scholastic Inc., 730 Broadway, New York, NY 10003.

ISBN 0-590-42189-1

Copyright © 1989 by Norman Bridwell.
All rights reserved. Published by Scholastic Inc.

12 11 10 9 8 7 6 5 4 3 2 1   9/8 0 1 2 3 4/9

Printed in the U.S.A.   23

First Scholastic printing, August 1989

Hi! We are Clifford and Emily Elizabeth.
Clifford is my dog. He's pretty big.

Clifford wasn't always so big.
When he was a puppy,
he was very, very small.

I had to be careful when I played with him.

He was too small to fetch a ball.

Poor little Clifford.

He wanted to play with my toys.

They were too big.

But he liked the merry-go-round I made for him.

On cold winter days, Clifford found snuggly warm places to sleep...

...like my cap.

We put a clock by his bed at night.
The ticking seemed to lull him to sleep.

Once I forgot to turn off the alarm.

At first I gave Clifford baths in our bathtub.

He slipped off the soap one day
and I almost lost him!

After that, I bathed him in a soup bowl.

Daddy was surprised when I told him
what I had used for Clifford's bathtub.

It was fun having such a small puppy.

But Clifford was easy to lose.

One day my aunt came to visit.

When she left, we looked all over
for our small red puppy.

My aunt found him in the bake shop.

Clifford was scared. He plopped into the cream puffs.

Then he ran through the pies.

The baker tried to catch him,
but Clifford climbed up the wedding cake...

...and landed in the whipped cream.

The baker was a little upset.

What a mess! My aunt didn't know what to do. She didn't want to bring Clifford home looking like that.

A small boy with a big dog had an idea.
He said his dog loved whipped cream.

In no time, Clifford was all cleaned up.

I was so happy to have Clifford home again. The dog who brought him to me was the biggest dog I had ever seen...

...until Clifford grew up.